# CHAMPIONS

*To Max JH*
*To my parents, Brenda and Ivan EQ*

Text copyright © Jonathan Harlen 1998
Illlustrations copyright © Emma Quay 1998

First published in 1998 by
Red Fox
(A Marc Macleod Book)
Random House Australia
an imprint of
Random House Australia Pty Ltd
20 Alfred Street, Milsons Point NSW 2061

First published in Great Britain in 1999 by
Macdonald Young Books
an imprint of
Wayland Publishers Ltd
61 Western Road
Hove
East Sussex BN3 1JD

A catalogue record for this book
is available from the British Library

ISBN 0 7500 2872 6

# CHAMPIONS

Jonathan Harlen ◆ Emma Quay

MACDONALD YOUNG BOOKS

If a tiger fought a stingray
On my *grandma's* double bed

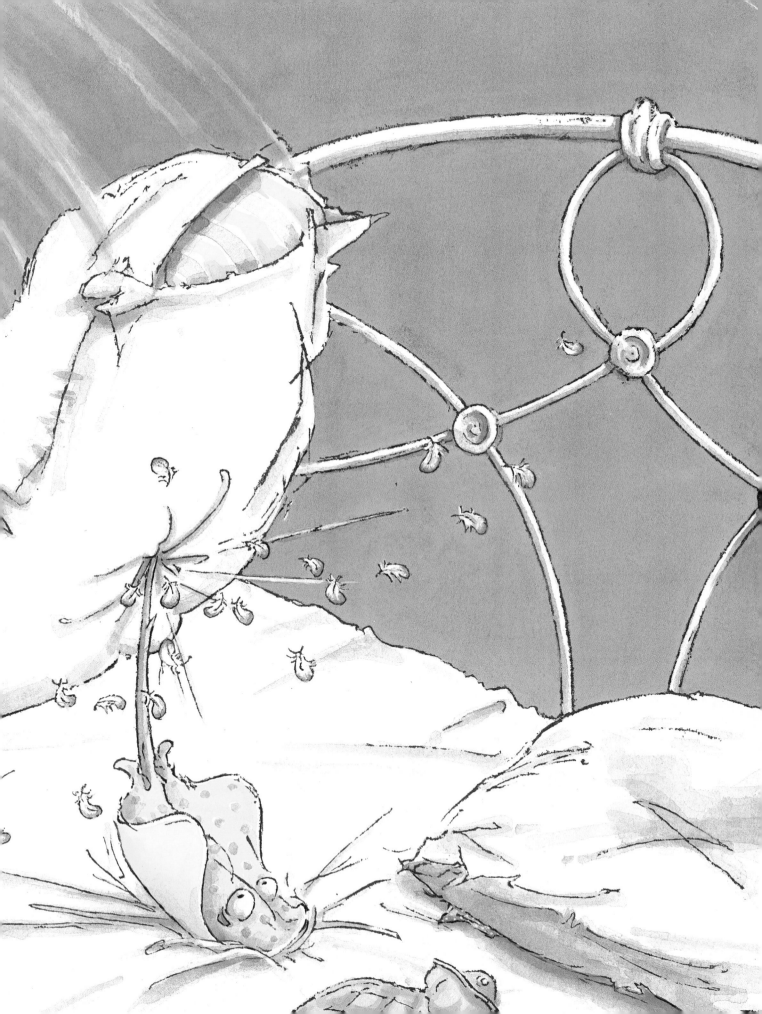

If a python fought a grizzly bear
Inside our garden shed

If an emu
fought a hippo
With a bucket on its head

Who would be the
**strongest**
of them all?

If the stingray
*raced* the
grizzly bear
Along the River Nile

If the tiger *raced* the emu
Through the city for a while

If the python *raced* the hippo
Down a supermarket aisle

Who would be the **fastest** of them all?

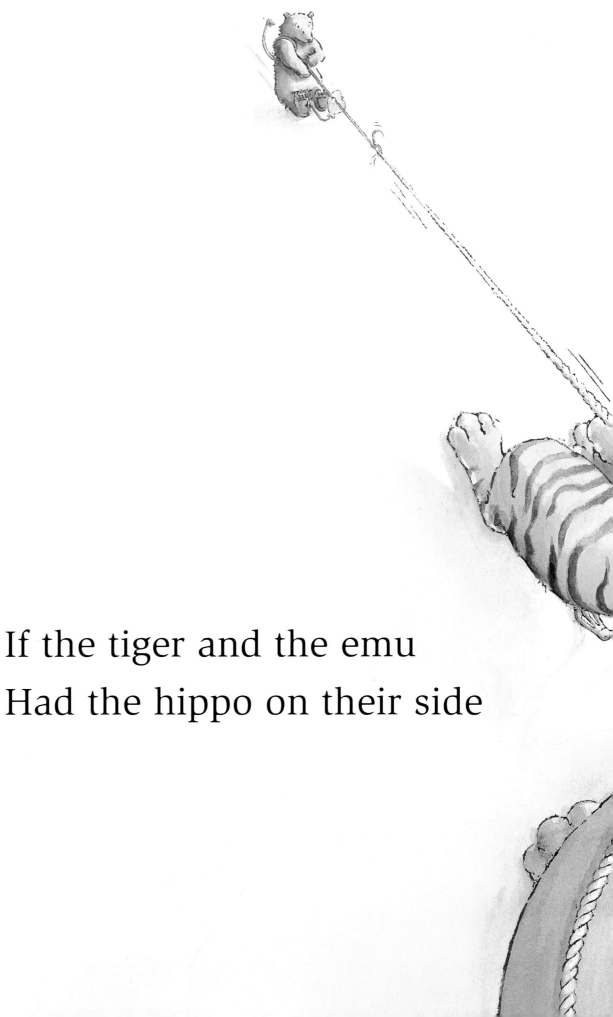

If the tiger and the emu
Had the hippo on their side

If the grizzly took the python
And the stingray for a *ride*.

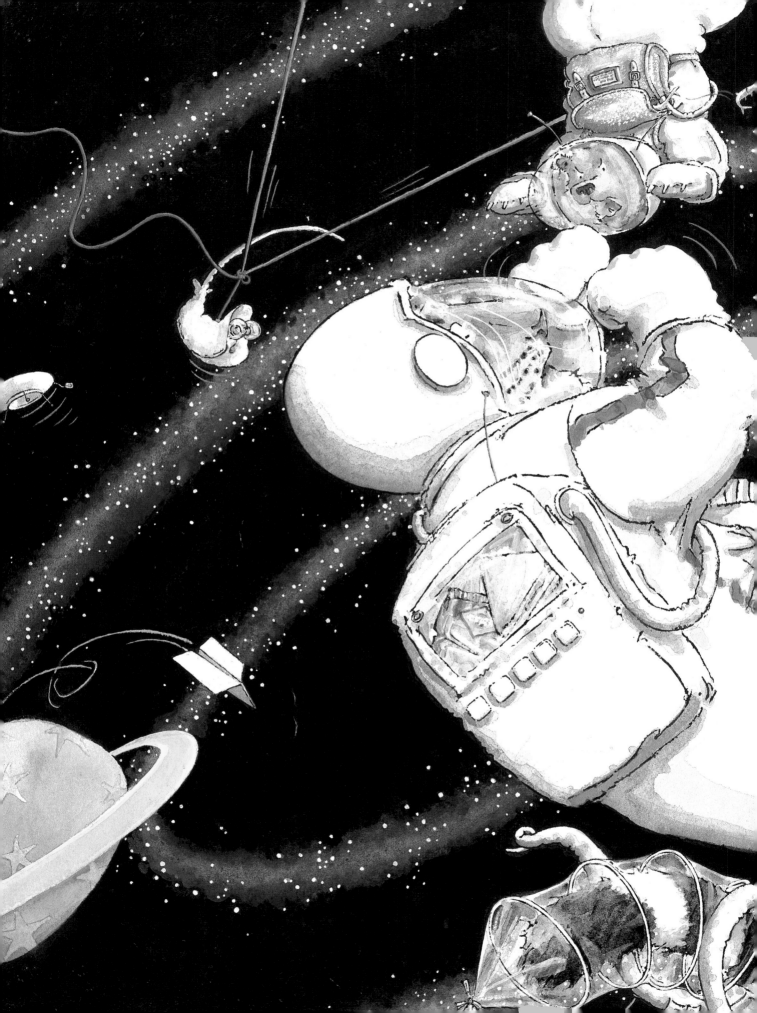

If they fought
in outer space
And the tiger *really tried*

Who would be the
**CHAMPION** of
them all?

The stingray is the champion
At *swimming* through a wave

The grizzly is the champion
At sleeping in a cave

The emu is the champion
At being very brave

And **Scaring** all the predators away

The tiger is the champion
At **hunting** late at night

The hippo is the champion
At sinking out of sight

# The python is the champion

At squeezing very tight

All of them are champions!

# Hooray!